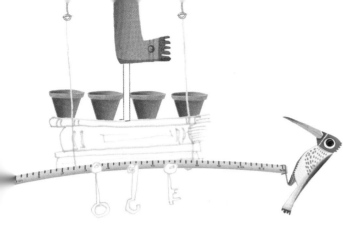
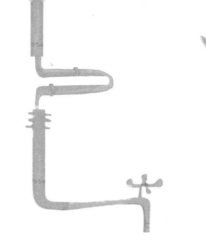

THiS
book
beLoNgs
to: ....

Dreams aRe like Acorns,
PLAnt thEM well, tend tHem
cArefully aNd theY will grow
to be As migHty as an Oak.

traditioNal Proverb

For GRandmA
aNd DaDa.

A TEMPLAR BOOK

First published in the UK in 2020 by Templar Publishing,
an imprint of Bonnier Books UK,
The Plaza, 535 King's Road, London, SW10 0SZ
www.templarco.co.uk
www.bonnierbooks.co.uk

Text and illustrations copyright © 2020 by Julia Patton
Design copyright © 2020 by Templar Books

10 9 8 7 6 5 4 3 2 1
All rights reserved

ISBN 978-1-78741-628-4

This book was typeset in The Hand
The illustrations were drawn in pencil, handmade
with collage papers and coloured digitally.

Edited by Katie Haworth
Designed by Genevieve Webster
Production by Neil Randles

Printed in Poland

No. 7

EVERGREEN
STREET

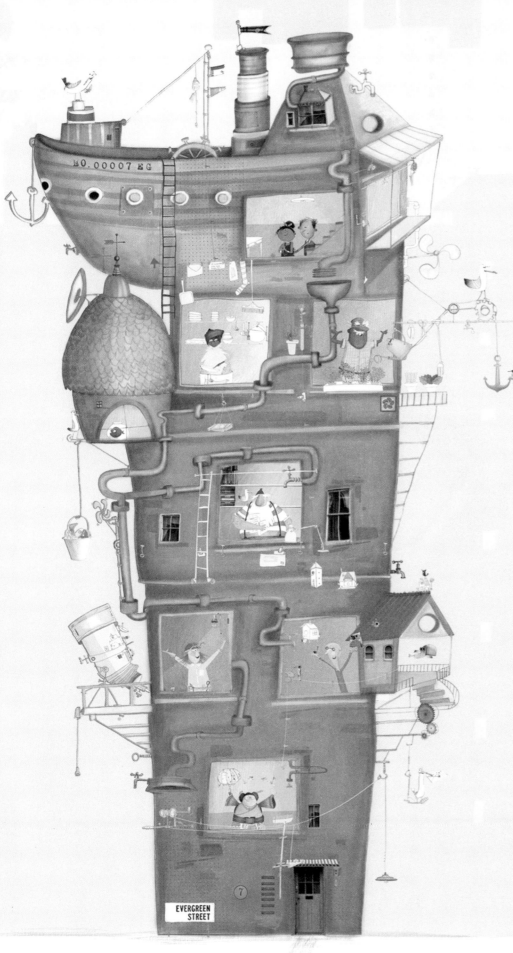

Number 7 Evergreen Street

Julia Patton

templar
books

Penelope Petersham

lived in a flat high in number 7 Evergreen Street.
Her name might have been Penelope,
but everyone called her Pea because she was tiny
and she loved wearing **green.**

Number 7 was an old, grey building . . .

. . . and Evergreen Street was an old, grey street.

coming soon

← NEW HOMES

Luxury
Flats!
COMING
SOON

EVERGREEN STREET

Pea had **never** seen anything growing there.

NEW HOMES

IS THIS YOUR DREAM HOME?

But inside number 7, it wasn't grey at all.

Pea had lived there since she was a baby, and she and her mum and dad knew all the residents.

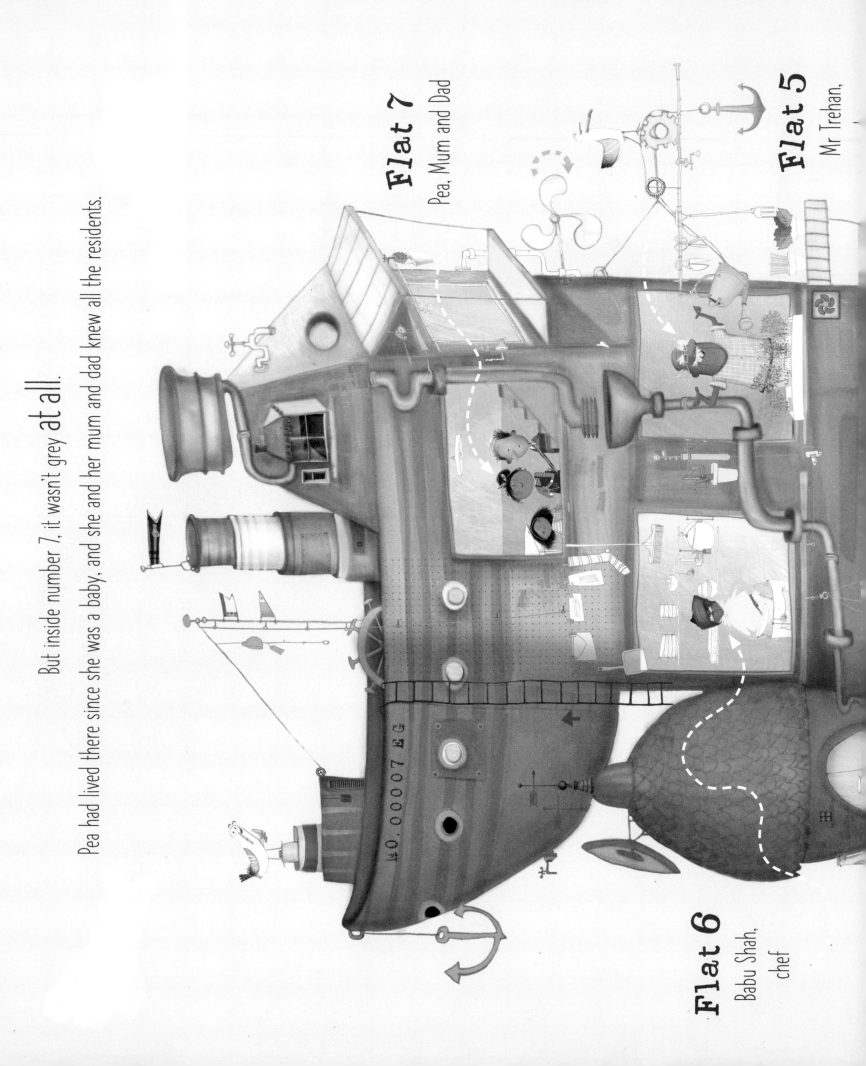

Flat 7
Pea, Mum and Dad

Flat 5
Mr Trehan,

Flat 6
Babu Shah,
chef

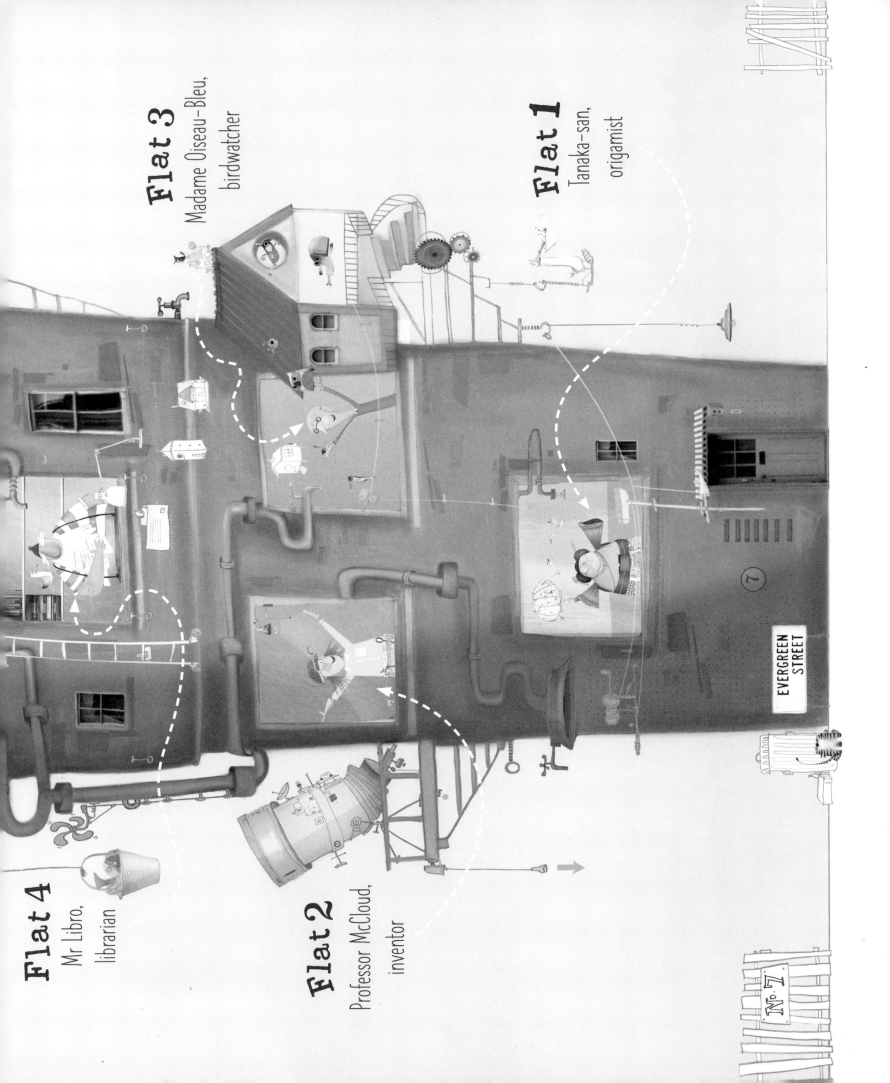

Flat 3
Madame Oiseau-Bleu, birdwatcher

Flat 1
Tanaka-san, origamist

Flat 4
Mr Libro, librarian

Flat 2
Professor McCloud, inventor

EVERGREEN STREET

No. 7

Over many years, number 7 Evergreen Street had been slowly adapted by the people inside, who used their building to communicate in a very special way. On a typical day:

1 Tanaka-san sent a paper-bird note to Professor McCloud.

2 Professor McCloud read it and had an idea for a new invention. She told Madame Oiseau-Bleu her idea . . .

3 . . . and Madame shouted the idea to Mr Libro . . . . . . over a **very noisy** toucan.

Mr Libro found some books for the professor . . . .

4 . . . and he lent books to Mr Trehan too.

Mr Trehan gave herbs to Babu Shah ...

5

6

...and Babu Shah made delicious samosas ...

...which he

delivered to Pea and her parents.

Pea's friends made every day together
exciting!

7

With love

TRADITIONAL INDIAN CUISINE

One rainy morning, Pea spotted something on Evergreen Street
that wasn't grey at all.

It was **yellow!**

EVERGREEN
STREET

The yellow things multiplied overnight and in the morning

an army of yellow workers covered the ground like bees.

Evergreen Street was even visited by the mayor, who made it very clear he had **big** plans.

Mayor's Big
BIG PLAN
No.7

No.8 No.9 10

I HAVE
BIG PLANS!

As more machines and workers arrived,
Pea asked lots of questions.

Why are
they here?

They're here
to build some
new flats.

Why do
we need more
flats?

So more families
have a home of their
own like you.

And she had **more** questions as she and her parents watched the workers swarm over the building site.

Who sent them?

Maybe the mayor, Pea. He's got BIG plans.

Every day, the new buildings grew bigger...

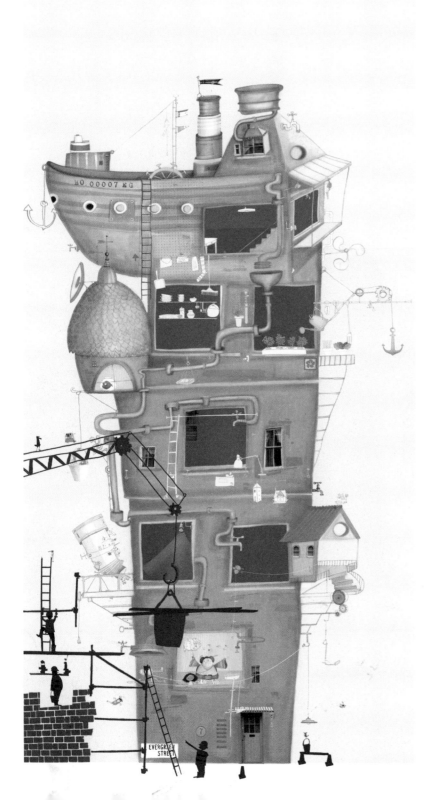

and bigger...

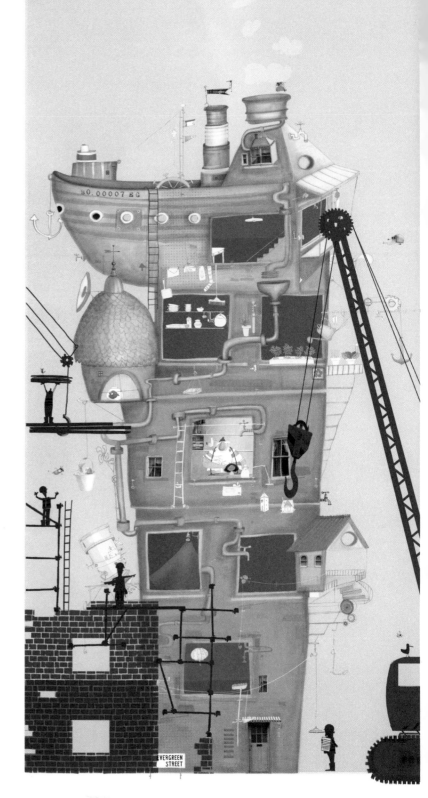

and bigger . . .

Until, finally, they were finished
and new people arrived in moving trucks.
Pea had even more questions then.

Who are they?

Can we meet them?

Maybe, Pea.

EVERGREEN STREET

7

VERY BIG & VERY IMPORTANT POST

TO THE RESIDENTS OF NO.7 EVERGREEN STREET.

Then, just when the residents of number 7 thought their street couldn't change any more, a **very important** letter was delivered.

Inside was the saddest news imaginable. The workers were going to tear down number 7 in three months' time, and every single one of them would have to leave.

This time Pea asked more questions than she ever had before . . .

What do we do now?

Will we still live with all our friends?

Where will we go?

. . . but her parents didn't seem to know the answers.

That evening, Pea's friend Mr Trehan brought her a gift, a tiny oak tree.
He explained that, like her, one day it would grow much, much bigger.

I hope your new home has a garden to plant it in.

THANK YOU!

Pea stared at the tiny oak tree
and imagined it big and tall and green . . .
and then something
really amazing happened.

OH!

Pea, the smallest person in number 7 Evergreen Street,
had the **biggest idea!**

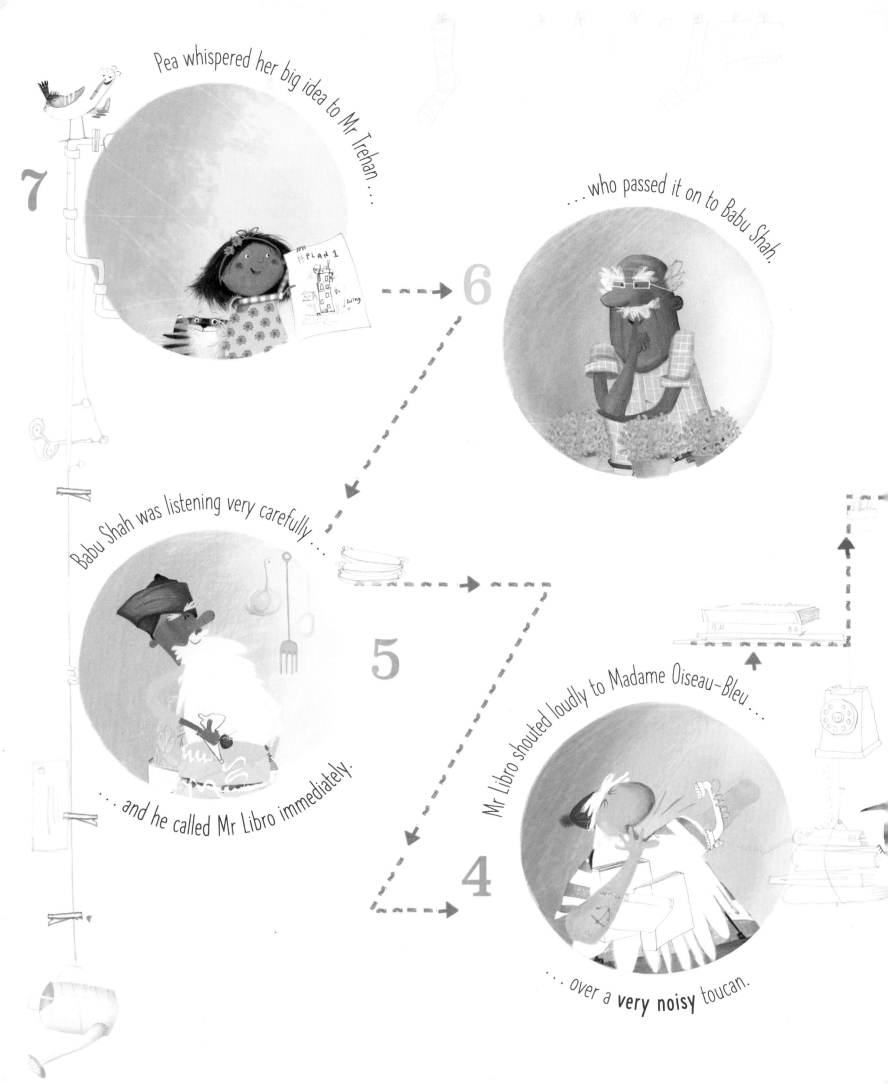

7 Pea whispered her big idea to Mr Trehan . . .

. . . who passed it on to Babu Shah.

6

Babu Shah was listening very carefully . . .

5

. . . and he called Mr Libro immediately.

Mr Libro shouted loudly to Madame Oiseau-Bleu . . .

4

. . . over a **very noisy** toucan.

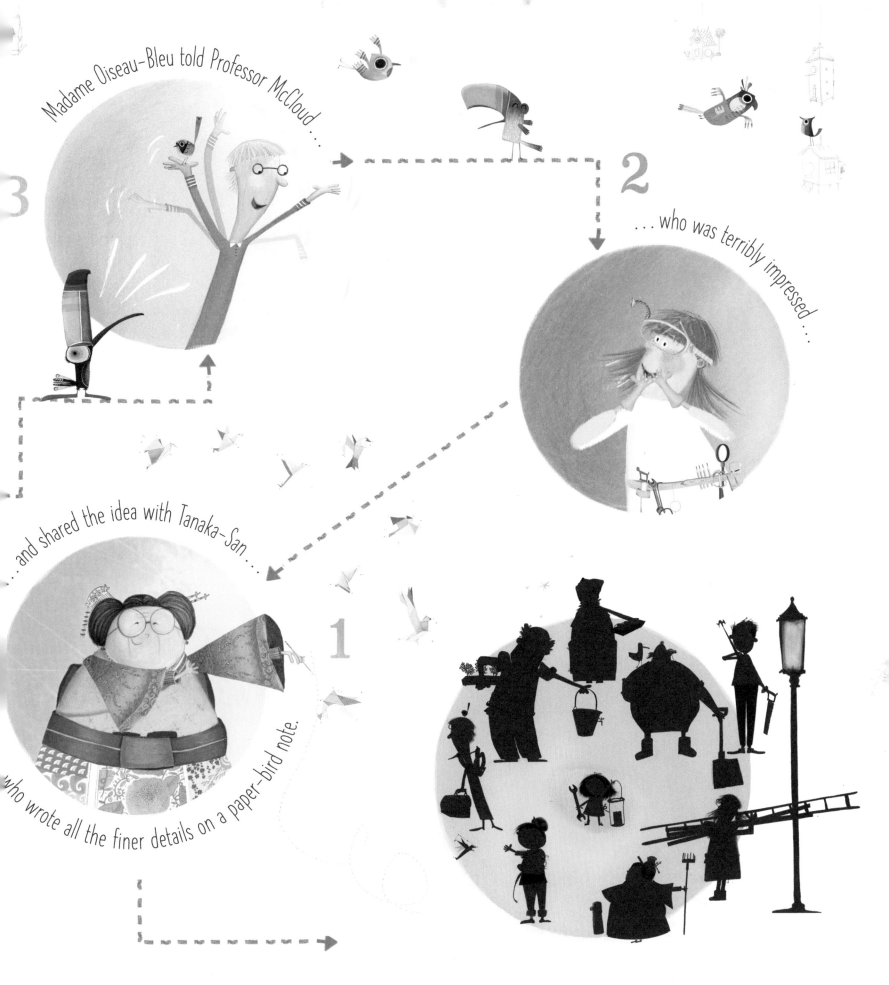

3 Madame Oiseau-Bleu told Professor McCloud...

2 ...who was terribly impressed...

...and shared the idea with Tanaka-San...

1 ...who wrote all the finer details on a paper-bird note.

That night when the lights went out on Evergreen Street, everyone gathered outside the building with spades, hammers, old bits of wood and everything else they needed.

In the morning, there was a tall fence all around
number 7 Evergreen Street.
When the mayor saw it, he just laughed.

YOU THINK YOUR
FLIMSY FENCE CAN STOP MY
BIG BULLDOZERS?

IN THREE MONTHS
THIS AWFUL OLD
BUILDING WILL COME
TUMBLING DOWN!

As the weeks went by, the new residents of Evergreen Street
sometimes stopped to look up at the fence.

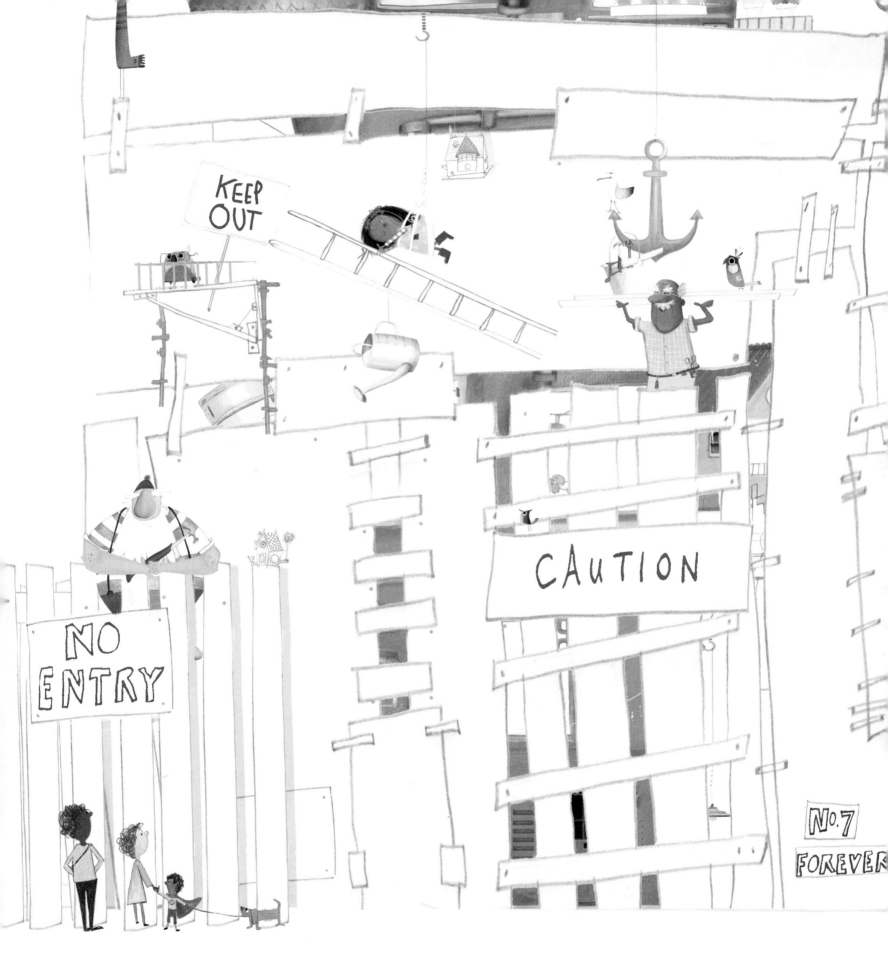

No one thought it would stop the bulldozers or the mayor. Rather strange noises were heard
from behind it, but no one could guess what was really going on.

Exactly three months later, the yellow army
returned bringing huge diggers, tall cranes
and a **very angry** mayor.

I DEMAND
YOU TAKE THIS
FENCE DOWN
AT ONCE!

Number 7 Evergreen Street was unrecognisable! Behind the fence, hidden from the eyes of the world, Pea and her family and friends had changed their home completely. It was now surrounded by

the most beautiful garden!

No.7

EVERGREEN
STREET

The mayor wasn't the only one with **big plans.**

Pea and all her friends excitedly explained what they'd been busy doing.
As for the mayor, his big demolition plans were finally over when he was handed
a petition signed by every person who lived on the street.

"Okay," said Pea. And so they did.

The mayor announced one last **big plan**.

I HAVE A BIG PLAN!

He said that number 7 should stay just as it was, so that families and friendships could blossom in the new garden. Everyone agreed this was the best plan he'd **ever** had!

Pea still lives in a flat in number 7 Evergreen Street,
but it's not a grey building anymore and it's no longer a grey street.
Now it's bursting with Penelope Petersham's favourite colour,

green!

No.7

EVERGREEN STREET

The
END

Bye!

More picture books from Templar:

ISBN: 978-1-78741-660-4 (paperback)
ISBN: 978-1-78741-565-2 (hardback)

ISBN: 978-1-78741-661-1

ISBN: 978-1-78741-473-0

ISBN: 978-1-78741-391-7